I0830780

# Looking-Glass House

# Looking-Glass House

*The Lost Manuscript of*
Through the Looking-Glass
*by Lewis Carroll*

Roverzone Press

FIRST AMERICAN EDITION

Published by Roverzone Press

roverzone@gmail.com

Book Design by Andrew Ogus

ISBN 978-0-692-70472-1

Manufactured in USA

Ingram Spark Print on Demand

# FOREWORD

Daniel Rover Singer

In the autumn of 2015, fans of Lewis Carroll celebrated the 150th anniversary of the publishing of *Alice's Adventures in Wonderland* all over the globe. I attended a whirlwind of gallery displays, multimedia presentations, discussions, and performances in New York City put on by the Lewis Carroll Society of North America, rubbing elbows with old friends and lots of odd strangers.

Did I say "odd?" Yes. Fans of Lewis Carroll are mostly odd creatures, drawn to the quirky weirdness of his ingenious nonsense. In addition to his famously strange books, Lewis Carroll remains a somewhat mystical personage, mainly because we have a hard time believing that a relatively straight-laced, 19th-century Oxford geometry teacher could write something as breathtakingly bizarre as *The Hunting of the Snark* or *Sylvie and Bruno*, let alone the most enduring, most quotable, and most surreal children's books of all time.

As I shopped in the Alice150 convention lobby, where vendors sold Lewis Carroll memorabilia of every description, I was surrounded by oddballs like me, purchasing books and trinkets and chatting away. At one table, I was fondling a new facsimile of *Alice's Adventures under Ground*, the celebrated rough-draft manuscript with Lewis Carroll's own amateurish yet fantastic illustrations.

"You like *Alice under Ground?*" said a soft, creaky voice. I looked up at the vendor, but clearly he had not spoken. I turned to find a delightfully eccentric old woman to my right. She had a wonderfully wrinkly, fuzzy face with glasses that made her twinkling eyes look huge. A gray shawl was wrapped loosely around her head, giving her an otherworldly appearance. She smiled and stared at me.

"Yes," I replied. "I love Carroll's original drawings."

"You LOVE them?"

"Yes," I laughed, "I love them, because we get to see what Carroll thought his *Wonderland* creatures looked like, before anybody else drew them – his raw, eccentric genius, scribbled right onto the pages. Also, I love it because it's a handmade labor-of-love that he gifted to his ideal child-friend. I love it because it symbolizes the connection that Carroll had with Alice Liddell; if she hadn't begged him to write the stories down, one of humanity's most enduring brands might have died like a summer daydream." I paused. "You probably think I'm a tremendous geek."

"Takes one to know one," she replied. "I've been standing by this table all day. No one seems as fond of *Alice under Ground* as you are. Can I show you something?"

"Of course."

"Where can we go? Somewhere private?"

I stared back at her. I was beginning to suspect this lady was weirder than most. I imagined she was going to try to sell me something. But I wasn't worried for my safety – if she attacked me, I was confident I could fend her off – you can't be too careful, meeting strangers in a big city, right? But I decided to humor her, and suggested we find a place to chat further.

She followed me out of the building. I pointed to a diner across the street. The old lady nodded in agreement. We crossed the street silently, went in, and sat in a booth. I told the waiter to give us a few minutes.

"I'm Rover," I said, introducing myself. "Are you a member of the Lewis Carroll Society?"

She shook her head and put a little parcel wrapped in brown paper on the table. "Open it," she told me.

I have to confess, even though I expected to find some tattered, mass-market copy of *Alice in Wonderland* that the old woman hoped might be worth $50, I couldn't help feeling a rush of expectation. You know how Charlie Bucket must have felt when he started to pull the wrapper off his chocolate bar, hoping for a Golden Ticket, in spite of knowing he'd never find one? I pulled the paper off, exposing a small book. It looked like one of the many reproductions of *Alice under Ground*, except that it looked vintage and slightly smudged. Hmm, I thought, not in good condition, but it might be worth something.

"Open it," she insisted.

That's when I noticed the title. Beautifully hand-painted on the cover were the words *Looking-Glass House*.

My heart skipped a beat, and then pounded in my chest. I felt my face blush red as the diner and the world around me spun into oblivion – all I could see were a strange old woman and a book.

I opened it. There was Lewis Carroll's unmistakable hand-printed lettering: "Chapter One: The Glass Curtain." And there was an illustration of Alice playing with her black kitten, instantly recognizable as Carroll's own wonderful, painstaking, scribbly hand. I flipped through several more pages, and there were his chessmen, his Jabberwock … drawings no one had ever seen before! And it wasn't a reproduction. It was the real thing. I thought I was having a heart attack.

The original *Under Ground* manuscript is in the British Library. It's one of their most prized artifacts. And here was its companion – the rough draft of *Through the Looking-Glass*, created sometime in the late 1860s but completely unknown and undiscovered.

"Is this real?" I murmured, fully knowing it was. She nodded. "Why do you have it?"

"It was handed down to me."

"Are you related to the Liddell family?"

"No. "

"How did you get this?"

She gathered her thoughts and took a deep breath. "When my mother was dying, she shoo'd everybody out of her bedroom except for me, and she gave me this book. She told me that her grandmother had been a child-friend of Lewis Carroll's, and that he wrote *Looking Glass House* for her."

My mouth was hanging open – like a codfish. "Lewis Carroll wrote this for your great-grandma?"

"Yes. My mother told me to keep it secret, and to pass it down to the next generation. But I don't have children to give it to. Do you want to buy it?"

"Ha! I mean, thank you, but this is probably worth millions," I whispered, suddenly aware that people might hear us.

"I was waiting to see who might want it. I wish to sell it to someone who will love it like my family always has."

"But you can sell it at auction. Seriously. I'm not rich."

"How much money do you have in your wallet? Cash?"

Incredulously, I pulled out my wallet, removed all the cash, and counted it. "Five hundred and forty dollars. I probably have some change too."

She plucked the cash from my hand without a moment's hesitation. "Keep the change," she smiled, "and someday, when you have to part with it, don't sell it to the highest bidder. Pass it on to someone who will love it as much as you do."

I reached for the book, but I suddenly didn't want to touch it, fearing that my sweaty hands would soil the cover. My mind swam with questions and concerns and possibilities. "Do you mind if I share this with the world?" I asked, looking up.

But there was no one sitting across from me; the old woman had gone. I scooped up the book and ran outside, but of course, she had disappeared onto the busy sidewalks of crowded Manhattan.

Looking-
Glass
House

# Chapter 1
# The Glass Curtain

One thing was certain: that the <u>white</u> kitten had had nothing to do with it—it was the black kitten's fault entirely. For Dinah, the old cat, had been washing the white kitten's face for the last quarter of an hour; so you see that it <u>couldn't</u> have had any hand in the mischief.

But the black kitten had been finished with earlier in the afternoon; and so, while Alice was sitting curled up in a corner of the great arm-chair, half talking to herself and half asleep, the kitten had been having a grand game of romps with the ball of worsted Alice had been trying to wind up, and had been rolling it up and down till it had all come undone again; and there it was, spread over the hearth-rug, all knots and tangles, with the kitten running after its own tail in the middle.

"Oh, you wicked little thing!" cried Alice, catching up the kitten, and giving it a little kiss to make it understand that it was in disgrace.

"Now let's have a serious game of chess, and you can be the Red Queen. I think if you sat up and folded your arms, you'd look exactly like her!"

Alice got the Red Queen off the  table, and set it before the kitten as a model for it to imitate: however, the thing didn't succeed, prin- -cipally, Alice said, because the kitten wouldn't fold its arms properly. To punish it, she held it up to the looking-glass above the chimney-piece, that it might see how sulky it was — "and if you're not good directly," she added, "I'll put you through into Looking-glass House. How would you like that?

"Now, if you'll attend, Kitty, I'll tell you all my ideas about Looking-glass House. First, there's the room you can see through the glass — that's just the same as our drawing room, only the things go the other way. I can see all of it when I get upon a chair — all but the bit behind the fireplace. Oh! I do so wish I could see that bit! I want so much to know whether they've a fire in the winter: you never can tell, you know, unless our fire smokes, and then smoke comes up in that room too—but that may be only pretence, just to make it look as if they had a fire. Well then, the books are something like our books, only the words go the wrong way; I know that, because I've held up one of our books to the glass, and then they hold up one in the other room.

"How would you like to live in Looking-glass House, Kitty? I wonder if they'd give you milk in there? Perhaps Looking-glass milk isn't good to drink — But oh, Kitty! now we come to the passage. You can just see a little peep of the passage in Looking-glass House, if you leave the door of our drawing-room wide open: and it's very like our passage as far as you can see, only you know it may be quite different on beyond. Oh, Kitty! how nice it would be if we could only get through into Looking-glass House! Let's pretend there's a way of getting through into it, somehow, Kitty! Let's pretend the glass has got all soft like a curtain, so that we can get through. Why, it's turning into a curtain now, I declare! It'll be easy enough to get through — " She was up on the chimney-piece while she said this, though she hardly knew how she had got there. And certainly the glass was beginning to part, just like the curtain on a stage.

In another moment Alice was through the glass, and had jumped lightly down into the Looking-glass room. The very first thing she did was to look whether there was a fire in the fireplace, and she was quite pleased to find that there was a real one, blazing away as brightly as the one she had left behind. "Oh, what fun it'll be, when they see me through the glass in here, and ca'n't get at me!"

Then she began looking about, and noticed that what could be seen from the old room was quite common and uninteresting, but that all the rest was as different as possible. For instance, the pictures on the wall next to the fire seemed to be all alive, and the very clock on the chimney-piece (you know you can only see the back of it in the looking--glass) had got the face of a little old man, and grinned at her.

"They don't keep this room so tidy as the other," Alice thought to herself, as she noticed several of the chessmen down in the

hearth among the cinders: but in another mo-
-ment, with a little "Oh!" of surprise,
she was down on her hands and knees watching
them. The chessmen were walking about, two and two!

"Here are the Red King and the Red
Queen," Alice said (in a whisper, for fear of
frightening them), "and there are the White
King and the White Queen sitting on the
edge of the shovel——and here are two
castles walking arm in arm——I don't think

they can hear me," she went on, as she put her head closer down, "and I'm nearly sure they ca'n't see me. I feel somehow as if I were invisible!"

There was a book lying near Alice on the table; she turned over the leaves, to find some part that she could read, "--- for it's all in some language I don't know," she said to herself.  She puzzled over this for some time, but at last a bright thought struck her. "Why, it's a Looking-glass book, of course! And if I hold it up to a glass, the words will all go the right way again."

This was the poem that Alice read. And you can read it yourself, the way Alice did, by holding this book up to a looking-glass.

"And hast thou slain the Jabberwock?
Come to my arms, my beamish boy!
O frabjous day! Callooh! Callay!"
He chortled in his joy

'Twas brillig, and ye slithy toves
Did gyre and gimble in ye wabe;
All mimsy were ye borogoves,
And ye mome raths outgrabe.

# JABBERWOCKY

'Twas brillig, and the slithy toves
Did gyre and gimble in the wabe;
All mimsy were the borogoves,
And the mome raths outgrabe.

"Beware the Jabberwock, my son!
The jaws that bite, the claws that catch!
Beware the Jubjub bird, and shun
The frumious Bandersnatch!"

He took his vorpal sword in hand:
Long time the manxome foe he sought—
So rested he by the Tumtum tree,
And stood awhile in thought.

And as in uffish thought he stood,
The Jabberwock, with eyes of flame,
Came whiffling through the tulgey wood,
And burbled as it came!

One, two! One, two! And through and through
The vorpal blade went snicker-snack!
He left it dead, and with its head
He went galumphing back.

"It seems very pretty," she said when she had finished it, "but it's _rather_ hard to understand! Somehow it seems to fill my head with ideas——only I don't exactly know what they are! However, _somebody_ killed _something_: that's clear, at any rate——

"But oh!" thought Alice, "if I don't make haste I shall have to go back through the Looking-glass, before I've seen what the rest of the house is like! Let's have a look at the garden first!"

She was out of the room in a moment, and ran downstairs——or, at least, it wasn't exactly running. She just kept the tips of her fingers on the hand-rail, and floated gently down without even touching the stairs with her feet; then she floated on through the hall, and would have gone straight out at the door in the same way, if she hadn't caught hold of the door-post. She was getting a little giddy with so much floating in the air, and was rather glad to find herself walking again in the natural way.

# Chapter II
# Garden of Live Flowers

"I should see the garden far better," said Alice to herself, "if I could get to the top of that hill: and here's a path that leads straight to it." Soon she came upon a large flower-bed, with a border of daisies, and a willow tree growing in the middle.

"O Tiger-lily," said Alice, addressing herself to one that was waving gracefully about in the wind, "I wish you could talk!"

"We _can_ talk," said the Tiger-lily: "when there's anybody worth talking to."

Alice was so astonished that she could not speak for a minute: it quite seemed to take her breath away. At length, as the Tiger-lily only went on waving about, she spoke again, in a timid voice—almost in a whisper.

14

"Can _all_ the flowers talk?"

"As well as _you_ can," said the Tiger-lily. "And a great deal louder."

"It isn't manners for us to begin, you know," said the Rose, "and I really was wondering when you'd speak! Said I to myself, 'Her face has got _some_ sense in it, though it's not a clever one!' Still, you're the right colour, and that goes a long way."

"I don't care about the colour," cried a Daisy. "If only her petals curled up a little more!" Here the daisies all began laughing at once, until Alice had to shout, "If you don't hold your tongues, I'll pick you!"

There was silence in a moment, and several of the pink daisies turned white.

"That's right!" said the Tiger-lily. "The daisies are worst of all. When one speaks, they all begin together, and it's enough to make one wither to hear the way they go on!"

"Are there any more people in the garden besides me?" Alice said.

"There's one other flower in the garden that can move about like you," said the Rose, "but she's more bushy than you are."

"She has the same awkward shape as you," the Daisy said, "but she's redder —— and her petals are shorter."

"Her petals are done up close, like a dahlia," the Tiger-lily interrupted: "not tumbled about anyhow, like yours."

"But that's not _your_ fault," the Rose added kindly: "you're beginning to fade, you know."

Alice didn't like this idea at all: so, to change the subject, she asked, "Does she ever come out here?"

"I daresay you'll see her soon," said the Rose.

"She's coming!" cried the Larkspur. "I hear her footstep along the gravel-walk!"

Alice looked round eagerly, and found that it was the Red Queen. "She's grown a good deal!" was her first remark. She had indeed: when Alice first saw her on the hearth, she had been only three inches high — and here she was, half a head taller than Alice herself!

"Where do you come from?" said the Red Queen. "And where are you going? Look up, speak nicely, and don't twiddle your fingers."

Alice attended to all these directions, and explained, as well as she could, that she had lost her way.

"I don't know what you mean by _your_ way," said the Queen: "all the ways about here belong to _me_ —— but why did you come out here at all?" she added in a kinder tone. "Curtsey while you're thinking what to say: it saves time."

Alice wondered a little at this, but she was too much in awe of the Queen to disbelieve it.

"It's time for you to answer now," the

Queen said, looking at her watch: "open your mouth a _little_ wider when you speak, and always say 'your Majesty.'"

"I only wanted to see what the garden was like, your Majesty——"

"That's right," said the Queen, patting her on the head, which Alice didn't like at all, "though, when you say 'garden,' I've seen gardens, compared with which this would be a wilderness."

Alice didn't dare to argue the point, but went on: "——and I thought I'd try and find my way to the top of that hill——"

"When you say 'hill,'" the Queen interrupted, "_I_ could show you hills, in comparison with which you'd call that a valley."

"No, I shouldn't," said Alice, surprised into contradicting her at last: "a hill ca'n't be a valley, you know. That would be nonsense——"

The Red Queen shook her head. "You may call it 'nonsense' if you like," she said, "but I've heard nonsense, compared with which that would be as sensible as a dictionary!"

Alice curtseyed again, as she was afraid from the Queen's tone that she was a _little_ offended: and they walked on in silence till they got to the top of the little hill.

For some minutes Alice stood without speaking, looking out in all directions over the country——and a most curious country it was. There were a number of tiny little brooks running straight across it from side to side, and the ground between was divided up into squares by a number of little green hedges, that reached from brook to brook.

"I declare it's marked out just like a large chess-board!" Alice said at last. "There ought to be some men moving about

somewhere—and so there are!" she added in a tone of delight, and her heart began to beat quick with excitement as she went on. "It's a great huge game of chess that's be- -ing played — all over the country! Oh, what fun! How I _wish_ I was one of them! I wouldn't mind being a Pawn, if only I might join —— though of course I should _like_ to be a Queen, best."

She glanced rather shyly at the real Queen as she said this, but her companion only smiled pleasantly, and said, "That's easily managed. You can be the White Queen's Pawn. You're in the Second Square to begin with; a pawn goes two squares in its first move, so you'll go very quickly through the Third Square—by railway, I should think—and when you get to the Eighth Square we shall be Queens together, and it's all feasting and fun!—" Just at this moment, somehow or other, they began to run.

Alice never could quite make out, in thinking it over afterwards, how it was that they began: all she remembers is, that they were running hand in hand, and the Queen went so fast that it was all she could do to keep up with her: and still the Queen kept crying "Faster! Faster!" but Alice felt she <u>could not</u> go faster, though she had not breath left to say so.

The most curious part of the thing was, that the trees and the other things round them never changed their places at all: however fast they went, they never seemed to pass anything. "I wonder if all the things move along with us?" thought poor puzzled Alice. And the Queen seemed to guess her thoughts, for she cried "Faster! Don't try to talk!"

Not that Alice had any idea of doing _that_. She felt as if she would never be able to talk again, she was getting so much out of breath: and still the Queen cried "Faster! Faster!" and dragged her along.

"Are we nearly there?" Alice managed to pant out at last.

"Nearly there!" the Queen repeated. "Why, we pass--ed it ten minutes ago! Faster!" And they ran on for a time in silence, with the wind whistling in Alice's ears, and almost blowing her hair off her head, she fancied.

"Now! Now!" cried the Queen. "Faster! Faster!" And they went so fast that at last they seemed to skim through the air, hardly touching the ground with their feet, till suddenly, just as Alice was getting quite exhausted, they stopped, and she found herself sitting on the ground, breathless and giddy.

The Queen propped her up against a tree, and said kindly, "You may rest a little now."

Alice looked round her in great surprise. "Why, I do believe we've been under this tree the whole time! Everything's just as it was!"

"Of course it is," said the Queen, "what would you have it?"

"Well, in _our_ country," said Alice, still panting a little, "you'd generally get to somewhere else — if you ran very fast for a long time, as we've been doing."

"A slow sort of country!" said the

Queen. "Now, _here_, you see, it takes all the running _you_ can do, to keep in the same place. If you want to get somewhere else, you must run at least twice as fast as that!"

"I'd rather not try, please!" said Alice. "I'm quite content to stay here—only I am so hot and thirsty!"

"I know what _you'd_ like!" the Queen said good-naturedly, taking a little box out of her pocket. "Have a biscuit?"

Alice thought it would not be civil to say "No," though it wasn't at all what she wanted. So she took it, and ate it as well as she could: it was _very_ dry; and she thought she had never been so nearly choked in all her life.

"Speak in French when you ca'n't think of the English for a thing," said the Queen, turning to go; "turn out your toes as you walk —— and remember who you are!"

Suddenly she was gone. Whether she vanished into the air, or whether she ran quickly into the wood ("and she _can_ run very fast!" thought Alice), there was no way of guessing, but she was gone; and Alice began to remember that she was a Pawn, and that it would soon be time for her to move.

# Chapter III
# Looking-Glass Insects

Alice ran down the hill and jumped over the first of the six little brooks.

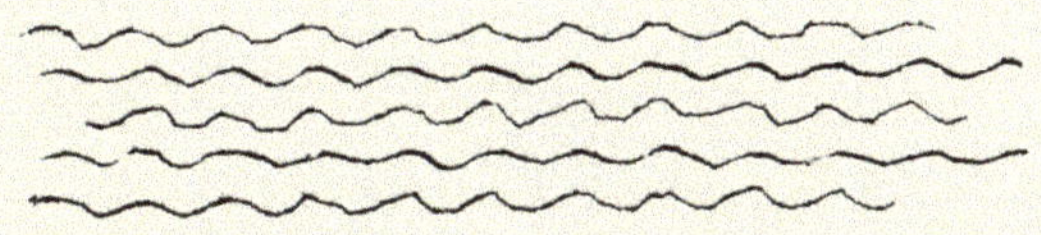

"Tickets, please!" said the Guard, putting his head in at the window. In a moment everybody was holding out a ticket: they were about the same size as the people, and quite seemed to fill the carriage.

"Now then! Show your ticket, child!" the Guard went on, looking angrily at Alice. And a great many voices all said together ("like the chorus of a song," thought Alice), "Don't keep him waiting, child! Why, his time is worth a thousand pounds a minute!"

"I'm afraid I haven't got one," Alice said in a frightened tone: "there wasn't a ticket-office where I came from." And again the chorus of voices went on. "There wasn't room for one where she came from. The land there is worth a thousand pounds an inch!"

"Don't make excuses," said the Guard: "you should have bought one from the engine--driver." And once more the chorus of voices went on with "The man that drives the engine. Why, the smoke alone is worth a thousand pounds a puff!"

Alice thought to herself, "Then there's no use in speaking." The voices didn't join in this time, as she hadn't spoken, but to her great surprise, they all <u>thought</u> in chorus (I hope you understand what <u>thinking in chorus</u> means— for I must confess that I don't), "Better say nothing at all. Language is worth a thousand pounds a word!"

"I shall dream about a thousand pounds to-night, I know I shall!" thought Alice.

All this time the Guard was looking

at her, first through a telescope, then through a microscope, and then through an opera-glass. At last he said, "You're travelling the wrong way," and shut up the window and went away.

"So young a child," said the gentleman sitting opposite to her (he was dressed in white paper), "ought to know which way she's going, even if she doesn't know her own name!"

A Goat, that was sitting next to the gentleman in white, shut his eyes and said in a loud voice, "She ought to know her way to the ticket-office, even if she doesn't know her alphabet!"

There was an old woman sitting next to the Goat, and, as the rule seemed to be that they should all speak in turn, she went on

with "She'll have to go back from here as luggage!"

Alice couldn't see who was sitting

beyond the old woman, but a hoarse voice spoke next. "Change engines——" it said. Suddenly a shrill scream came from the engine, and everybody jumped up in alarm, Alice among the rest.

A horse, who had put his head out of the window, quietly drew it in and said, "It's only a brook we have to jump over." Everybody seemed satisfied with this, though Alice felt a little nervous at the idea of trains jump- -ing at all. "However, it'll take us into the Fourth Square, that's some comfort!" she said to herself. In another moment she felt the carriage rise straight up into the air, and in her fright she caught at the thing nearest to her hand, which happened to be the old woman's hair.

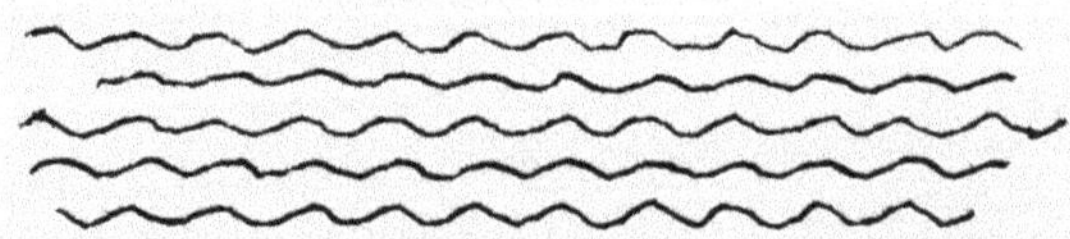

But the hair seemed to melt away as she touched it, and thump! down Alice came upon a soft field of grass. The train had vanished, and Alice found herself under a tree near a very old man (only that his face was more like a wasp), all huddled up together, and shivering as if he were very cold.

"Oh, my old bones, my old bones!" he was grumbling as Alice came up to him.

"It's rheumatism, I should think," Alice said to herself, and she stooped over him, and said very kindly, "I hope you're not in much pain?"

The Wasp only shook his shoulders, and turned his head away. "Ah, deary me!" he said to himself.

"I'm afraid you're not well," she said in a soothing tone. "Ca'n't I do anything for you?"

"It's all along of the wig," the Wasp said in a much gentler voice.

"Along of the wig?" Alice repeated.

"You'd be cross too, if you'd a wig like mine," the Wasp

went on. "They jokes at one. And they worrits one. And then I gets cross. And I gets cold. And I gets under a tree. And I gets a yellow handkerchief. And I ties up my face — as at the present."

He untied the handkerchief as he spoke, and Alice looked at his wig in great surprise. It was bright yellow like the handkerchief, and all tangled and tumbled about like a heap of seaweed. "You could make your wig much neater," she said, "if only you had a comb."

"What, you're a Bee, are you?" the Wasp said, looking at her with more interest. "And you've got a comb. Much honey?"

"It isn't that kind," Alice hastily explained. "It's to comb hair with—your wig's so <u>very</u> rough, you know; and it doesn't fit you well at all."

"What sort of insects do you rejoice in?" the Wasp inquired, suddenly changing the subject.

"I don't <u>rejoice</u> in insects at all," Alice explained, "because I'm rather afraid of them—at least the large kinds. Do you rejoice in insects?"

"Halfway up that bush, you'll see a Rocking-Horse-Fly. It's made of wood, and swings itself from branch to branch."

"What does it live on?" Alice asked with great curiosity.

"Sap and sawdust," said the Wasp. "And crawling at your feet, you may observe a Bread-a-Butter-Fly. Its wings are thin slices of bread-a-butter, its body is a crust, and its head is a lump of sugar."

"And what does _it_ live on?"

"Weak tea with cream in it."
"Supposing it couldn't find any?" she suggested.

"Then it would die, of course."

The two sat quietly pondering for a minute. "Your wig fits very well," the Wasp murmured at last, looking at Alice with an expression of admiration: "it's the shape of your head as does it. Your jaws ain't well shaped, though —I should think you couldn't bite well?"

Alice gave a little scream of laughter, then managed to say gravely, "I can bite anything I want."

"Not if you was a-fighting," the Wasp persisted. "How could you get hold of the other one by the back of the neck?"

"Well, I'm afraid I couldn't," Alice replied.

"That's because your jaws are too short. And your eyes—they're too much in front. One would have done as well as two, if you _must_ have them so close."

Alice did not like having so many personal remarks made on her, and as the Wasp had quite recovered his spirits, she thought she might safely leave him. "I think I must be going on now," she said. "Good-bye."

"Good-bye, and thank-ye," said the Wasp.

Alice remembered that she was now in the Fourth Square, and that she must hurry on with the game. She soon came to an open field, with a wood on the other side of it: it looked much darker than the last wood, and Alice felt a little timid about going into it. "Which of these finger-posts ought I to follow, I wonder?"

It was not a very difficult question to answer, as there was only one road through the wood, and the two finger-posts both pointed along it. "I'll settle it," Alice said to herself, "when the road divides and they point different ways."

But this did not seem likely to happen. Wherever the road divided there were sure to be two finger-posts pointing the same way, marked

"I ca'n't stay there long. I'll just call and say, 'How d'you do?' and ask them the way out of the wood. If I could only get to the Eighth Square before it gets dark!" So she wandered on, talking to herself as she went, till, on turning a sharp corner, she came upon two fat little men, so suddenly that she could not help starting back, but in another moment she recovered herself, feeling sure that they must be

# Chapter IV
# Tweedledum & Tweedledee

They were standing under a tree, each with an arm round the other's neck, and Alice knew which was which in a moment, because one of them had "DUM" embroidered on his collar, and the other "DEE." "I suppose they've each got "TWEEDLE" round at the back of the collar," she said to herself.

They stood so still that she quite forgot they were alive, and she was just looking round to see if the word "TWEEDLE" was written at the back of each collar, when she was startled by a voice coming from the one marked "DUM."

"If you think we're wax-works," he said, "you ought to pay, you know. Wax-works weren't made to be looked at for nothing, nohow!"

"Contrariwise," added the one marked "DEE," "if you think we're alive, you ought to speak."

"I'm sure I'm very sorry," was all Alice could say; for the words of the old song kept ringing through her head like the ticking of a clock, and she could hardly help saying them out loud: —

"Tweedledum and Tweedledee
Agreed to have a battle;
For Tweedledum said Tweedledee
Had spoilt his nice new rattle.

Just then flew down a monstrous crow,
As black as a tar-barrel;
Which frightened both the heroes so,
They quite forgot their quarrel."

"I know what you're thinking about," said Tweedledum: "but it isn't so, nohow."

"Contrariwise," continued Tweedledee, "if it was so, it might be; and if it were so, it would be; but as it isn't, it ain't. That's logic."

"I was thinking," Alice said very politely, "which is the best way out of this wood: it's getting so dark. Would you tell me, please?"

But the little men only looked at each other and grinned.

They looked so exactly like a couple of great schoolboys, that Alice couldn't help pointing her finger at Tweedledum, and saying "First Boy!"

"Nohow!" Tweedledum cried out briskly, and shut his mouth up again with a snap.

"Next Boy!" said Alice, passing on to Tweedledee, though she felt quite certain he would only shout out "Contrariwise!" and so he did.

"You've begun wrong!" cried Tweedledum. "The first thing in a visit is to say 'How d'ye do?' and shake hands!" And here the two brothers gave each other a hug, and then they held out the two hands that were free, to shake hands with her.

Alice did not like shaking hands with either of them first, for fear of hurting the other one's feelings; so, as the best way out of the difficulty, she took hold of both hands at once: the next moment they were dancing round in a ring. This seemed quite natural (she remembered afterwards), and she was not even surprised to hear music playing: it seemed to come from the tree under which they were dancing, and it was done (as well as she could make it out) by the branches rubbing one across the other, like fiddles and fiddle-sticks.

The other two dancers were fat, and very soon out of breath. "Four times round is enough for one dance," Tweedledum panted out, and they left off dancing as suddenly as they had begun: the music stopped at the same moment.

"I hope you're not much tired?" Alice said at last.

"Nohow. And thank you _very_ much for asking," said Tweedledum.

"So _much_ obliged!" added Tweedledee.

Alice was quite alarmed to hear something that sounded to her like the puffing of a large steam-engine in the wood near them, though she feared it was more likely to be a wild beast. "Are there any lions or tigers about here?" she asked timidly.

"It's only the Red King snoring," said Tweedledee.

"Come and look at him!" the brothers cried, and they each took one of Alice's hands, and led her up to where the King was sleeping.

"Isn't he a _lovely_ sight?" said Tweedledum.

Alice couldn't say honestly that he was. He had a tall red night-cap on, with a tassel, and he was lying crumpled up into a sort of untidy heap, and snoring loud—"fit to snore his head off!" as Tweedledum remarked.

"He's dreaming now," said Tweedledee: "and what do you think he's dreaming about?"

Alice said, "Nobody can guess that."

"Why, about <u>you</u>!" Tweedledee exclaimed, clapping his hands triumphantly. "And if he left off dreaming about you, where do you suppose you'd be?"

"Where I am now, of course," said Alice.

"Not you!" Tweedledee retorted contempt-uously. "You'd be no-where. Why, you're only a sort of thing in his dream!"

"If that there King was to wake," added Tweedledum, "you'd go out—bang!— just like a candle!"

"I shouldn't!" Alice exclaimed indignantly. "Besides, if I'm only a sort of thing in his dream, what are <u>you</u>, I should like to know?"

"Ditto!" said Tweedledum.

"Ditto, ditto!" cried Tweedledee.

He shouted this so loud that Alice couldn't help saying, "Hush! You'll be waking him, if you make so much noise."

"Well, it's no use <u>your</u> talking about waking him," said Tweedledum, "when you're only one of the things in his dream. You know very well you're not real."

"I _am_ real!" said Alice and began to cry.

"You won't make yourself a bit realler by crying," Tweedledee remarked.

"If I wasn't real," Alice said—half-laughing through her tears, it all seemed so ridiculous—"I shouldn't be able to cry."

"I hope you don't suppose those are _real_ tears?" Tweedledum interrupted in a tone of great contempt.

"I know they're talking nonsense," Alice thought to herself: "and it's foolish to cry about it." So she brushed away her tears, and went on as cheerfully as she could. "At any rate I'd better be getting out of the wood, for really it's coming on very dark. Do you think it's going to rain?"

Tweedledum spread a large umbrella over himself and his brother. "No, I don't think it is," he said: "at least ——not under _here_. Nohow."

"But it may rain _outside_?"

"It may—if it chooses," said Tweedledee: "we've no objection. Contrariwise."

"Selfish things!" thought Alice, and she was just going to leave them, when Tweedledum sprang out from under the umbrella and seized her by the wrist.

"Do you see _that?_" he said, in a voice choking with passion, as he pointed with a trembling finger at a small white thing lying under the tree.

"It's only a rattle," Alice said, after a careful examination. "Not a rattle-_snake_, you know," she added hastily: "only an old rattle—quite old and broken."

"But it _isn't_ old!" cried Tweedledum, beginning to stamp about wildly and tear his hair. "I bought it yesterday, and now it's spoi_lt_! _My nice new rattle!_" Here he looked at Tweedledee, who immediately sat down on the ground, and tried to hide himself under the umbrella. "Of course you agree to have a battle?" Tweedledum said in a calmer tone.

"I suppose so," the other sulkily replied, as he crawled out of the umbrella, "but I don't care about going on long. What's the time now?"

Tweedledee looked at his watch, and said "Half-past four."

"Let's fight till six, and then have dinner," said Tweedledum.

"Very well," the other said, rather sadly.

"And all about a rattle!" said Alice, hoping to make them a _little_ ashamed of fighting for such a trifle.

"I shouldn't have minded it so much," said Tweedledum, "if it hadn't been a new one."

"I wish the monstrous crow would come!" thought Alice.

"There's only one sword, you know,"

Tweedledum said to his brother: "but you can have the umbrella—it's quite as sharp. Only we must begin quick. It's getting as dark as it can."

"And darker," said Tweedledee.

It was getting dark so suddenly that Alice thought there must be a thunderstorm coming on. "What a thick black cloud that is!" she said. "And how fast it comes! Why, I do believe it's got wings!"

"It's the crow!" Tweedledum cried out in a shrill voice of alarm: and the two brothers took to their heels and were out of sight in a moment.

Alice ran a little way into the wood, and stopped under a large tree. "It can never get at me <u>here</u>," she thought: "it's far too large to squeeze itself in among the trees. But I wish it wouldn't flap its wings so—it makes quite a hurricane in the wood — here's somebody's shawl being blown away!

# Chapter V
# Living Backwards

She caught the shawl as she spoke, and looked about for the owner: in another moment the White Queen came running wildly through the wood, with both arms stretched out wide, as if she were flying, and Alice very civilly went to meet her with the shawl.

"I'm very glad I happened to be in the way," Alice said, as she helped her to put on her shawl again.

The White Queen only looked at her in a helpless, frightened sort of way, and kept repeating something in a whisper to herself that sounded like "bread-and-butter, bread-and-butter," and Alice felt that if

there was to be any conversation at all, she must manage it herself. So she began rather timidly: "Am I addressing the White Queen?"

"Well, yes, if you call that a-dressing," the Queen said. "It isn't _my_ notion of the thing, at all."

Alice thought it would never do to have an argument at the very beginning of their conversation, so she smiled and said, "If your Majesty will only tell me the right way to begin, I'll do it as well as I can."

"But I don't want it done at all!" groaned the poor Queen. "I've been a-dressing myself for the last two hours."

It would have been all the better, as it seemed to Alice, if she had got someone else to dress her, she was so dreadfully untidy. "Every single thing's crooked," Alice thought to herself, "and she's all over pins!—— May I put your shawl straight for you?" she added aloud. "And, dear me, what a state your hair is in!"

"The brush has got entangled in it!" the Queen said with a sigh. "And I lost the comb yesterday."

Alice carefully released the brush, and did her best to get the hair into order. "Come, you look rather better now!" she said, after altering most of the pins. "But really you should have a lady's maid!"

"I'm sure I'll take _you_ with pleasure!" the Queen said. "Twopence a week, and jam every other day."

Alice couldn't help laughing, as she said, "I don't want you to hire _me_——and I don't care for jam."

"It's very good jam," said the Queen.

"Well, I don't want any to-day, at any rate."

"You couldn't have it if you _did_ want it," the Queen said. "The rule is, jam to-morrow and jam yesterday——but never jam to-day."

"It _must_ come sometimes to 'jam to-day,'" Alice objected.

"No, it ca'n't," said the Queen. "It's jam every _other_ day: to-day isn't any _other_ day, you know."

"I don't understand you," said Alice. "It's dreadfully confusing!"

"That's the effect of living backwards," the Queen said kindly: "it always makes one a little giddy at first——" But here the Queen began screaming so loud that she had to leave the sentence unfinished. "Oh, oh, oh!" shouted the Queen, shaking her hand about as if she wanted to shake it off. "My finger's bleeding! Oh, oh, oh, oh!"

Her screams were so exactly like the whistle of a steam-engine, that Alice had to hold both her hands over her ears.

"What _is_ the matter?" she said, as soon

as there was a chance of making herself heard. "Have you pricked your finger?"

"I haven't pricked it yet," the Queen said, "but I soon shall — oh, oh, oh!"

"When do you expect to do it?" Alice asked, feeling very much inclined to laugh.

"When I fasten my shawl again," the poor Queen groaned out: "the brooch will come undone directly. Oh, oh!" As she said the words the brooch flew open, and the Queen clutched wildly at it, and tried to clasp it again.

"Take care!" cried Alice. "You're holding it all crooked!" And she caught at the brooch; but it was too late: the pin had slipped, and the Queen had pricked her finger.

"That accounts for the bleeding, you see," she said to Alice with a smile. "Now you understand the way things happen here."

"But why don't you scream now?" Alice asked, holding her hands ready to put over her ears again.

"Why, I've done all the screaming already,"

said the Queen. "What would be the good of having it all over again? There goes the shawl again!"

The brooch had come undone as she spoke, and a sudden gust of wind blew the Queen's shawl across a little brook. The Queen spread out her arms again, and went flying after it, and this time she succeeded in catching it for herself. "I've got it!" she cried in a triumphant tone. "Now you shall see me pin it on again, all by myself!"

"Then I hope your finger is better now?" Alice said very politely, as she crossed the little brook after the Queen.

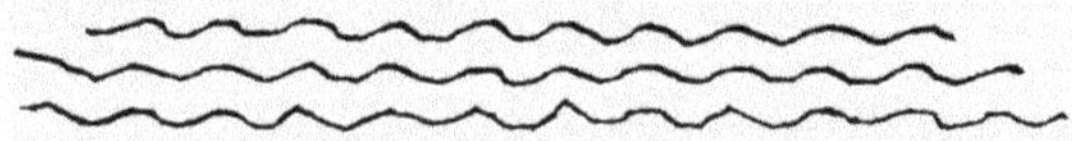

"Oh, much better!" cried the Queen, her voice rising to a squeak as she went on. "Much be-etter! Be-etter! Be-e-e-etter! Be-e-ehh!" The last word ended in a long bleat, so like a sheep that Alice quite started.

She looked at the Queen, who seemed

to have suddenly wrapped herself up in wool. Alice rubbed her eyes, and looked again. She couldn't make out what had happened at all. Was she in a shop? And was that really a _sheep_ sitting on the other side of the counter? Rub as she could, she could make nothing more of it: she was in a little dark shop, leaning with her elbows on the counter, and opposite to her was an old Sheep, sitting in an arm-chair knitting, and every now and then leaving off to look at her through a great pair of spectacles.

"What is it you want to buy?" the Sheep said at last, looking up for a moment from her knitting. She was working with fourteen pairs at once, and Alice couldn't help looking at her in great astonishment.

"How _can_ she knit with so many?" the puzzled child thought to herself. "She gets more and more like a porcupine every minute!"

"Can you row?" the Sheep asked, handing her a pair of knitting-needles as she spoke.

"Yes, a little—but not on land—and

not with needles—" Alice was beginning to say, when suddenly the needles turned into oars in her hands, and she found they were in a little boat, gliding along between banks: so there was nothing for it but to do her best.

"Oh, please! There are some scented rushes!" Alice cried in a sudden transport of delight. "There really are—and such beauties!"

So the boat was left to drift down the stream as it would, till it glided gently in among the waving rushes. And then the little sleeves were carefully rolled up, and the little arms were plunged in elbow-deep to get the rushes a good long way down before breaking them off—and for a while Alice forgot all about the Sheep, as she bent over the side of the boat, with just the ends of her tangled hair dipping into the water — while with bright eager eyes she caught at one bunch after another of the darling scented rushes.

"The prettiest are always further!" she said at last, with a sigh at the obstinacy of the rushes in growing so far off, as, with flushed cheeks and dripping hair and hands, she began to arrange her new-found treasures.

What mattered it to her just then that the rushes had begun to fade, and to lose all their scent and beauty, from the very moment that she picked them? Even real scented rushes, you know, last only a very little while—and these, being dream-rushes, melted away almost like snow, as they lay in heaps at her feet.

They hadn't gone much farther before the blade of one of the oars got fast in the water and wouldn't come out again; and the consequence was that the handle of it caught her under the chin, and, in spite of a series of little shrieks of "Oh, oh, oh!" from poor Alice, it swept her straight off the seat, and down among the heap of rushes.

However, she wasn't hurt, and was

soon up again: the Sheep went on with her knitting all the while, just as if nothing had happened.

"Now make up your mind, please," said the Sheep. "What _do_ you want to buy?"

"To buy!" Alice echoed in a tone that was half astonished and half frightened—for the oars, and the boat, and the river, had vanished all in a moment, and she was back again in the little dark shop.

"I should like to buy an egg, please," she said timidly, taking a coin from her pocket.

The Sheep took the money and put it away in a box: then she said, "I never put things into people's hands—that would never do—you must get it for yourself." And so saying, she went off to the other end of the shop, and set the egg upright on a shelf.

"I wonder _why_ it wouldn't do?" thought Alice, as she groped her way among the tables and chairs, for the shop was very dark towards the end. "The egg seems to get further away the more I walk towards it. Let me see, is this a chair? Why, it's got branches, I declare! How very odd to find trees growing here! And actually here's a little brook! Well, this is the very queerest shop I ever saw!"

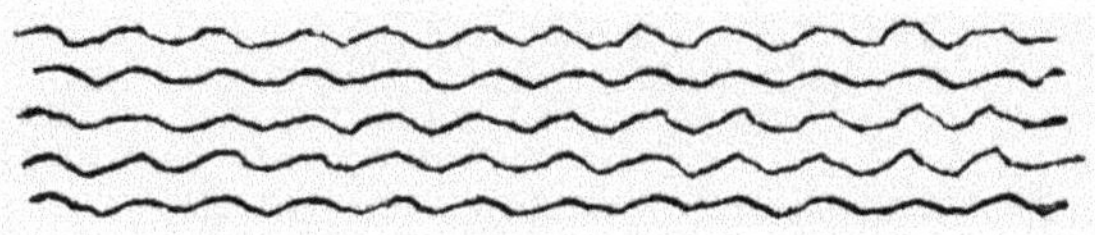

# Chapter VI
# Humpty Dumpty

The egg got larger and larger, and more and more human: when she had come within a few yards of it, she saw that it had eyes and a nose and mouth; and when she had come close to it, she saw clearly that it was HUMPTY DUMPTY himself.

Humpty Dumpty was sitting with his legs crossed, like a Turk, on the top of a high wall—such a narrow one that Alice quite wondered how he could keep his balance.

"And how exactly like an egg he is!" she said aloud.

"It's _very_ provoking," Humpty Dumpty said after a long silence, "to be called an egg—_Very_!"

"I said you <u>looked</u> like an egg, Sir," Alice gently explained. "And some eggs are very pretty, you know," she added, hoping to turn her remark into a sort of a compliment.

"Some people," said Humpty Dumpty, looking away from her as usual, "have no more sense than a baby!"

Alice didn't know what to say to this—— so she softly repeated to herself:——

"Humpty Dumpty sat on a wall:
Humpty Dumpty had a great fall.
All the King's horses and all the
 King's men
Couldn't put Humpty Dumpty in his
 place again."

"Don't stand there chattering to yourself like that," Humpty Dumpty said, looking at her for the first time, "but tell me your name and your business."

"My <u>name</u> is Alice, but ——"

"It's a stupid enough name!" Humpty Dumpty interrupted impatiently. "What does it mean?"

"Must a name mean something?" Alice asked doubtfully.

"Of course it must," Humpty Dumpty said with a short laugh: "my name means the shape I am—and a good handsome shape it is, too. With a name like yours, you might be any shape, almost."

"Why do you sit out here all alone?" said Alice, not wishing to begin an argument.

"Why, because there's nobody with me!" cried Humpty Dumpty. "Did you think I didn't know the answer to that? Ask another."

"Don't you think you'd be safer down on the ground?" Alice went on. "That wall is so very narrow!"

"What tremendously easy riddles you ask!" Humpty Dumpty growled out. "Of course I don't think so! Why, if ever I did fall off — which there's no chance of—but if I did fall," he went on, "The King has promised me—with his very own mouth—to — to—"

"To send all his horses and all his men," Alice interrupted.

"Now I declare that's too bad!" Humpty Dumpty cried. "You've been listening at doors— and behind trees— and down chimneys— or you couldn't have known it!"

"I haven't, indeed!" Alice said very gently. "It's in a book."

"Ah, well! They may write such things in a _book_," Humpty Dumpty said in a calmer tone. "That's what you call a History of England, that is. However, this conversation is going on a little too fast: let's go back to the last remark but one."

"I'm afraid I ca'n't quite remember it," Alice said very politely.

"In that case we start fresh," said Humpty Dumpty, "and it's my turn to choose a subject——" ("He talks about it just as if it was a game!" thought Alice.) "So here's a question for you. How old did you say you were?"

"Seven years and six months."

"Wrong!" Humpty Dumpty exclaimed triumphantly. "You never said a word like it! Seven years and six months," he repeated thoughtfully. "An uncomfortable sort of age. Now if you'd asked _my_ advice, I'd have said 'Leave off at seven'——but it's too late now."

"What a beautiful belt you've got on!" Alice suddenly remarked. "At least," she corrected herself on second thoughts, "a beautiful cravat, I should have said——no, a belt, I mean——I beg your pardon!" she added in dismay, for Humpty Dumpty looked thoroughly offended, and she began to wish she hadn't chosen that subject. "If I only knew," she thought to herself, "which was neck and which was waist!"

"It is a——most——provoking——thing," he said at last, "when a person doesn't know a cravat from a belt! It's a cravat, child, and a beautiful one, as you say. It's a present from the White King and Queen. They gave it me——for an un-birthday present."

"I like birthday presents best," Alice said.

"You don't know what you're talking about!" cried Humpty Dumpty. "How many days are there in a year?"

"Three hundred and sixty-five," said Alice.

"And how many birthdays have you?"

"One."

"And if you take one from three hundred and sixty-five, what remains?"

"Three hundred and sixty-four, of course."

"Well, that shows that there are three hundred and sixty-four days when you might get un-birthday presents——and only one for birthday presents, you know. There's glory for you!"

"I don't know what you mean by 'glory,'" Alice said.

Humpty Dumpty smiled contemptuously. "Of course you don't——till I tell you. I meant 'there's a nice knock-down argument for you!'"

"But 'glory' doesn't mean 'a nice knock-down argument,'" Alice objected.

"When _I_ use a word," Humpty Dumpty said in rather a scornful tone, "it means just what I choose it to mean——neither more nor less."

"The question is," said Alice, "whether you _can_ make words mean so many different things."

"The question is," said Humpty Dumpty, "which is to be Master——that's all. Good-bye!"

This was rather sudden, Alice thought: but, after such a _very_ strong hint that she ought to be going, she felt that it would hardly be civil to stay. So she held out her hand. "Good-bye, till we meet again!" she said as cheerfully as she could.

"I shouldn't know you again if we _did_ meet," Humpty Dumpty replied in a discontented tone, giving her one of his fingers to shake; "you're so exactly like other people."

"The face is what one goes by, generally," Alice remarked in a thoughtful tone.

"That's just what I complain of," said Humpty Dumpty. "Your face is the same as everybody has——the two eyes, so——" (marking their places in the air with this thumb) "nose in the middle, mouth under. It's always the same. Now if you had the two eyes on the same side of the nose, for instance——or the mouth at the top——that would be _some_ help.

"It wouldn't look nice," Alice objected. But Humpty Dumpty only shut his eyes and said "Wait till you've tried."

Alice waited a minute to see if he would speak again, but as he never opened his eyes or took any further notice of her, she said "Good-bye!" once more, and, getting no answer to this, she quietly walked away: but she couldn't help saying to herself as she went, "Of all the unsatisfactory people I _ever_ met——" She never finished the sentence, for at this moment a heavy crash shook the forest from end to end.

# Chapter VII
# The Lion & The Unicorn

The next moment soldiers came running through the wood, in such crowds that they seemed to fill the whole forest.

Alice got behind a tree, for fear of being run over, and watched them go by.

She thought that in all her life she had never seen soldiers so uncertain on their feet: they were always tripping over something or other, and whenever one went down, several more always fell over him, so that the ground was soon covered with little heaps of men.

Then came the horses. Having four feet, these managed rather better than the foot-soldiers: but even _they_ stumbled now and then; and it seemed to be a regular rule that, whenever a horse stumbled the rider fell off instantly. The confusion got worse every moment, and Alice was very glad to get out of the wood into an open place, where she found the White King seated on the ground, busily writing in a memorandum-book.

"I've sent them all!" the King cried in a tone of delight, on see- -ing Alice. "Did you happen to meet any soldiers, my dear, as you came through the wood?"

"Yes, I did," said Alice: "several thousand, I should think."

"Four thousand two hundred and seven, that's the exact number," the King said, referring to his book. "I couldn't send all the horses, you know, because two of them are wanted in the game. And I haven't sent my two Messengers, either. They're both gone to the town. Just look along the road, and tell me if you can see either of them."

"I see nobody on the road," said Alice.

"I only wish _I_ had such eyes," the King remarked in a fretful tone. "To be able to see Nobody! And at that distance, too! Why, it's as much as I can do to see real people, by this light!"

All this was lost on Alice, who was still looking intently along the road, shading her eyes with one hand. "I see somebody now!" she exclaimed at last.

At this moment the Messenger arrived: he was far too much out of breath to say a word, and could only wave his hands about, and make the most fearful faces at the poor King.

"This is Haigha," the King said, introducing Alice in the hope of turning off the Messenger's attention from himself——his attitudes got more extraordinary every moment, and his great eyes rolled wildly from side to side.

"You alarm me!" said the King. "Who did you pass on the road?"

"Nobody," said the Messenger.

"Quite right," said the King: "this young lady saw him too. So of course Nobody walks slower than you."

"I do my best," the Messenger said in a sulky tone. "I'm sure nobody walks much faster than I do!"

"He ca'n't do that," said the King, "or else he'd have been here first. However, now you've got your breath, you may tell us what's happened in the town."

"I'll whisper it," said the Messenger, putting his hands to his mouth in the shape of a trumpet, and stooping so as to get close to the King's ear. However, instead of whispering, he simply shouted at the top of his voice "They're at it again!"

"Do you call _that_ a whisper?" cried the poor King, jumping up and shaking himself.

"If you do such a thing again, I'll have you buttered! It went through and through my head like an earthquake!"

"Who are at it again?" Alice ventured to ask.

"Why the Lion and the Unicorn, of course," said the King, "fighting for the crown. And the best of the joke is, that it's _my_ crown all the while! Let's run and see them." And they trotted off, Alice repeating to herself, as she ran, the words of the old song:——

> "The Lion & the Unicorn
> Were fighting for the crown:
> The Lion beat the Unicorn
> All round the town.
> Some gave them white bread,
> Some gave them brown;
> Some gave them plum-cake
> And drummed them out of town."

They ran till they came in sight of a great crowd, in the middle of which the Lion and Unicorn were fighting. They placed themselves close to where Hatta, the King's other Messenger, was standing watching the fight.

"How are they getting on?" asked the King.

"Very well," Hatta said: "each of them has been down about eighty-seven times."

There was a pause in the fight just then, and the Lion and the Unicorn sat down, panting, while the King called out "Ten minutes allowed for refreshments!" Haigha and Hatta set to work at once, carrying trays of white and brown bread.

"I don't think they'll fight any more to-day," the King said to Hatta: "go and order the drums to begin." And Hatta went bounding away like a grasshopper.

At this moment the Unicorn sauntered by them, with his hands in his pockets. He stood for some time looking at Alice with an air of the deepest disgust.

"What—is—this?" he said at last.

"This is a child!" Haigha replied eagerly. "We only found it to-day. It's as large as life, and twice as natural!"

"I always thought they were fabulous monsters!" said the Unicorn. "Is it alive?"

"It can talk," said Haigha, solemnly.

The Unicorn looked dreamily at Alice, and said "Talk, child."

Alice could not help her lips curling up into a smile as she began: "Do you know, I always thought Unicorns were fabulous monsters, too! I never saw one alive before!"

"Well, now that we _have_ seen each other," said the Unicorn, "if you'll believe in me, I'll believe in you. Is that a bargain?"

"Yes, if you like," said Alice.

"Come, fetch out the plum-cake, old man!" the Unicorn went on, turning from her to the King. "None of your brown bread for me!"

"Certainly—certainly!" the King mut-
-tered, and beckoned to Haigha. "Open the
bag!" he whispered.

Haigha took a large cake out of his
bag, and gave it to Alice to hold, while he
got out a dish and carving-knife. How they
all came out of it Alice couldn't guess. It
was just like a conjuring-trick, she thought.

The Lion had joined them while this
was going on: he looked very tired and sleepy,
and his eyes were half shut. "What's this!"
he said, blinking lazily at Alice, and speaking
in a deep hollow tone that sounded like the
tolling of a great bell.

"Ah, what _is_ it, now?" the Unicorn
cried eagerly. "You'll never guess! I couldn't."

The Lion looked at Alice wearily.

"Are you animal — vegetable — or
mineral?" he said, yawning at every other
word.

"It's a fabulous monster!" the Unicorn
cried out, before Alice could reply.

"What a time the Monster is, cutting
up that cake!" growled the Lion.

Alice had seated herself on the bank of a little brook, with the great dish on her knees, and was sawing away diligently with the knife. "It's very provoking!" she said, "I've cut several slices already, but they always join on again!"

"You don't know how to manage Looking-glass cakes," the Unicorn remarked. "Hand it round first, and cut it afterwards."

This sounded nonsense, but Alice very obediently got up, and carried the dish round, and the cake divided itself into three pieces as she did so. "Now cut it up," said the Lion, as she returned to her place with the empty dish.

"I say, this isn't fair!" cried the Unicorn, as Alice sat with the knife in her hand, very much puzzled how to begin. "The Monster has given the Lion twice as much as me!"

"She's kept none for herself, anyhow," said the Lion. "Do you like plum-cake, Monster?"

But before Alice could answer him, the drums began.

Where the noise came from, she couldn't make out: the air seemed full of it, and it rang through and through her head till she felt quite deafened. She started to her feet and sprang across the little brook in her terror —

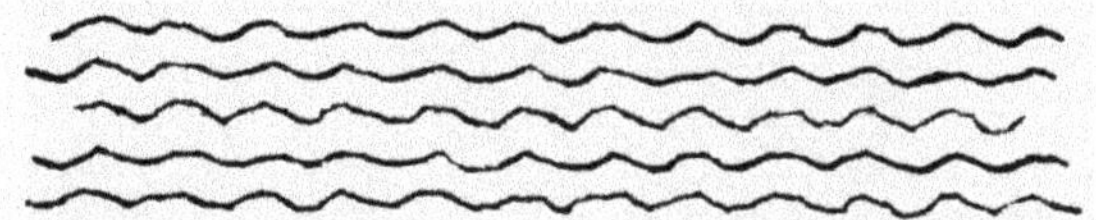

and had just time to see the Lion and the Unicorn rise to their feet, with angry looks at being interrupted in their feast, before she dropped to her knees, and put her hands over her ears, vainly trying to shut out the dreadful uproar.

"If _that_ doesn't 'drum them out of town,'" she thought to herself, "nothing ever will!"

# Chapter VIII
# Check!

After a while the noise seemed gradually to die away, till all was dead silence, and Alice lifted up her head in some alarm. There was no one to be seen, and her first thought was that she must have been dreaming about the Lion and the Unicorn and the King's Messengers. However, there was the great dish still lying at her feet, on which she had tried to cut the plum-cake, "So I wasn't dreaming, after all," she said to herself, "unless—unless we're all part of the same dream. Only I do hope it's _my_ dream, and not the Red King's! I don't like belonging to another person's dream," she went on in a rather complaining tone:

"I've a great mind to go and wake him, and see what happens!"

At this moment her thoughts were interrupted by a loud shouting of "Ahoy! Ahoy! Check!" and a Knight dressed in crimson armour came galloping down upon her, brandishing a great club. Just as he reached her, the horse stopped suddenly: "You're my prisoner!" the Knight cried, as he tumbled off his horse.

Startled as she was, Alice was more frightened for him than for herself at the moment, and watched him with some anxiety as he mounted again. As soon as he was comfortably in the saddle, he began once more "You're my——" but here another voice broke in "Ahoy! Ahoy! Check!" and Alice looked round in some surprise for the new enemy.

This time it was a White Knight. He drew up at Alice's side, and tumbled off his horse just as the Red Knight had done: then he got on again, and the two Knights sat and looked at each other.

"She's _my_ prisoner, you know!" the Red Knight said at last.

"Yes, but then _I_ came and rescued her!" the White Knight replied.

"Well, we must fight for her, then," said the Red Knight, as he took up his helmet (which hung from the saddle, and was something the shape of a horse's head), and put it on.

"You will observe the Rules of Battle, of course?" the White Knight remarked, putting on his helmet too.

"I always do," said the Red Knight, and they began banging away at each other with such fury that Alice got behind a tree to be out of the way of the blows.

"I wonder, now, what the Rules of Battle are," she said to herself, as she watched the fight, timidly peeping out from her hiding--place: "one Rule seems to be, that if one Knight hits the other, he knocks him off his horse, and if he misses, he tumbles off himself—and another Rule seems to be that they hold their clubs with their arms, as if they were Punch and Judy." Another Rule of Battle, that Alice had not noticed, seemed to be that they always fell on their heads, and the battle ended with their both falling off in this way, side by side: when they got up again, they shook hands, and then the Red Knight mounted and galloped off.

"It was a glorious victory, wasn't it?" said the White Knight, as he came up panting.

"I don't know," Alice said doubtfully. "I don't want to be anybody's prisoner. I want to be a Queen."

"So you will, when you've crossed the next brook," said the White Knight. "I'll see you safe to the end of the wood—and then I must go back, you know. That's the end of my move."

"Thank you very much," said Alice. "May I help you off with your helmet?" It was evidently more than he could manage by himself; however, she managed to shake him out of it at last.

"Now one can breathe more easily," said the Knight, putting back his shaggy hair with both hands, and turning his gentle face and large mild eyes to Alice. She thought she had never seen such a strange-looking soldier in all her life.

He was dressed in tin armour, which seemed to fit him very badly, and he had a queer-shaped  little deal-box fastened across his shoulder, upside-down, and with the lid hang-ing open. Alice looked at it with great curiosity.

"I see you're admiring my little box," the Knight said in a friendly tone. "It's my own invention—to keep clothes and sandwiches in. You see I carry it upside-down, so that the rain ca'n't get in."

"But the things can get <u>out</u>," Alice gently remarked. "Do you know the lid's open?"

"I didn't know it," the Knight said, a shade of vexation passing over his face. "Then all the things must have fallen out! And the box is no use without them." He unfastened it as he spoke, and was just going to throw it into the bushes, when a sudden thought seemed to strike him, and he hung it carefully on a tree. "Can you guess why I did that?" he said to Alice.

Alice shook her head.

"In hopes some bees may make a nest in it——then I should get the honey."

"But you've got a bee-hive——or something like one—fastened to the saddle," said Alice.

"Yes, it's a very good bee-hive," the Knight said in a discontented tone: "but not a single bee has come near it yet. And the other thing is a mouse-trap. I suppose the mice keep the bees out —— or the bees keep the mice out, I don't know which."

"I was wondering what the mouse-trap

was for," said Alice. "It isn't very likely there would be any mice on the horse's back."

"Not very likely, perhaps," said the Knight: "but if they _do_ come, I don't choose to have them running all about. You see," he went on after a pause, "it's as well to be provided for _everything_. That's the reason the horse has all those anklets round his feet."

"But what are they for?" Alice asked in a tone of great curiosity.

"To guard against the bites of sharks," the Knight replied. "It's an invention of my own."

For a few minutes they walked on, every now and then Alice stopping to help the poor Knight, who certainly was _not_ a good rider.

Whenever the horse stopped (which it did very often), he fell off in front; and whenever it went on again (which it generally did rather suddenly), he fell off behind. Otherwise he kept on pretty well, except that he had a habit of now and then falling off sideways; and as he generally did this on the side on which Alice was walking, she soon found that it was the best plan not to walk quite close to the horse.

"I'm afraid you've not had much practice in riding," she ventured to say, as she was helping him up from his fifth tumble.

The Knight looked very much surprised, and a little offended at the remark. "What makes you say that?" he asked, as he scrambled back into the saddle, keeping hold of Alice's hair with one hand, to save himself from falling over on the other side.

"Because people don't fall off quite so often, when they've had much practice."

"I've had plenty of practice," the Knight said very gravely: "plenty of practice!"

Alice could think of nothing better to say than "Indeed?" but she said it as heartily as she could.

"The great art of riding," said the Knight, "is to keep your balance properly. Like this, you know——"

He let go the bridle, and stretched out both his arms to show Alice what he meant, and this time he fell flat on his back, right under the horse's feet.

"Plenty of practice!" he went on repeating, all the time that Alice was getting him on his feet again. "Plenty of practice!"

"It's too ridiculous!" cried Alice, losing all her patience this time. "You ought to have a wooden horse on wheels, that you ought!"

"Does that kind go smoothly?" the Knight asked in a tone of great interest.

"Much more smoothly than a live horse," Alice said, with a little scream of laughter, in spite of all she could do to prevent it.

"Here I must leave you," said the Knight as they came to the end of the wood. "You've only a few yards to go, down the hill and over that little brook, and then you'll be a Queen——But you'll stay and see me off first?" he added as Alice turned with an eager look in the direction to which he pointed. "I shan't be long. You'll wait and wave your handkerchief when I get to that turn in the road? I think it'll encourage me."

"Of course I'll wait," said Alice: "and thank you very much for coming so far."

So they shook hands, and then the Knight rode slowly away into the forest. "It won't take long to see him _off_, I expect," Alice said to herself, as she stood watching him. "There he goes! Right on his head as usual!" So she went on talking to herself, as she watched the horse walking leisurely along the road, and the Knight tumbling off, first on one side and then on the other. After the fourth or fifth tumble he reached the turn, and then she waved her handkerchief to him, and waited till he was out of sight.

"I hope it encouraged him," she said, as she turned to run down the hill: "And now for the last brook, and to be a Queen! How grand it sounds!" A very few steps brought her to the edge of the brook: and she was just going to spring over, when she heard a deep sigh, which seemed to come from the wood behind her.

"There's somebody very unhappy there," she thought, looking anxiously back to see what was the matter. She saw the old Wasp sitting with his wings against a tree. "How can he have gotten to the Seventh Square so quickly?" Alice wondered, walking towards him.

"I took the train," sighed the Wasp, just as if Alice had spoken aloud. "How did you go?"

"I walked," said Alice. "In the Fourth Square I met Tweedledum and Tweedledee. In the Fifth Square I visited the queerest little shop——with a stream running down the middle of it."

"What did you buy?" asked the Wasp. "Any brown sugar?"

"I bought an egg, but it turned into Humpty Dumpty."

"Humph!" growled the Wasp, "no brown sugar!"

"In the Sixth Square," Alice went on, "The Lion and the Unicorn were fighting for the crown. The Unicorn thought I was a fabulous monster!"

"I did too!" said the Wasp, his eyes open wide with astonishment.

"The Red Knight tried to 'check' me in the Seventh Square, but the White Knight rescued me — and then fell off his horse," she added, with a smile. "And now, I'm about to become a Queen!"

"Well get on with ye then, and good luck," said the Wasp. Alice curtseyed politely, then tripped down the hill, quite pleased that she had given a few minutes to cheering up the miserable old creature.

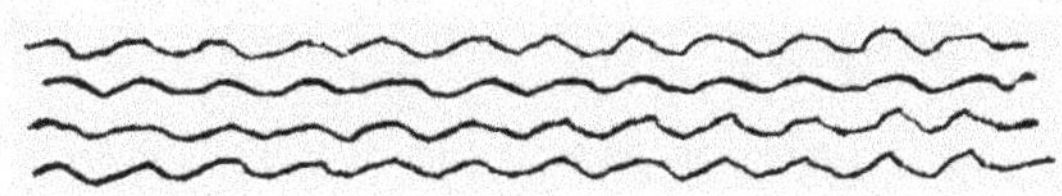

"The Eighth Square at last!" she cried as she bounded across the final brook and threw herself down to rest on the grass. "Oh, how glad I am to get here! And what is this on my head?" she exclaimed in a tone of dismay, as she put her hands up to something very heavy, and fitted tight all round her head.

It was a golden crown.

# Chapter IX
# Queen Alice

"Well, this _is_ grand!" said Alice. "I never expected I should be a Queen so soon!"

Everything was happening so oddly that she didn't feel a bit surprised at finding the Red Queen and the White Queen sitting close to her, one on each side. "Please, would you tell me if the game is over?" she began, looking timidly at the Red Queen.

"Speak when you're spoken to!" said the Red Queen sharply.

"But if everybody obeyed that rule," said Alice, "nobody would ever say anything."

"Ridiculous!" cried the Red Queen. "You

ca'n't be a Queen, you know, till you've passed the proper examination." Then there was an uncomfortable silence for a minute or two.

The Red Queen broke the silence by saying to the White Queen, "I invite you to Alice's dinner-party this afternoon."

The White Queen smiled feebly, and said "And I invite _you_."

"I didn't know I was to have a party at all," said Alice; "but if there _is_ to be one, I think _I_ ought to invite the guests."

"We gave you the opportunity of doing it," the Red Queen remarked: "but I daresay you've not had many lessons in manners yet?"

"Manners are not taught in lessons," said Alice. "Lessons teach you to do sums, and things of that sort."

"Can you do Addition?" the White Queen asked. "What's one and one and one and one and one and one and one and one and one and one?"

"I don't know," said Alice. "I lost count."

"She ca'n't do Addition," the Red Queen

interrupted. "Can you do Subtraction? Take nine from eight."

"Nine from eight? I ca'n't, you know," Alice replied very readily: "but——"

"She ca'n't do Subtraction," said the White Queen. "Can you do Division? Divide a loaf by a knife——what's the answer to _that?_"

"I suppose——" Alice was beginning, but the Red Queen answered for her. "Bread-and-butter, of course. Try another Subtraction sum. Take a bone from a dog: what remains?"

Alice considered. "The bone wouldn't remain, of course, if I took it——and the dog wouldn't remain; it would come to bite me —— and I'm sure _I_ shouldn't remain!"

"Then you think nothing would remain?" said the Red Queen.

"I think that's the answer."

"Wrong, as usual," said the Red Queen: "the dog's temper would remain."

"But I don't see how ——"

"Why, look here!" the Red Queen cried. "The dog would lose its temper, wouldn't it?"

"Perhaps it would," Alice replied cautiously.

"Then if the dog went away, its temper would remain!" the Queen exclaimed triumphantly.

Alice said, as gravely as she could, "They might go different ways." But she couldn't help thinking to herself, "What dreadful nonsense we _are_ talking!"

"She ca'n't do sums a _bit_!" the Queens said together, with great emphasis.

"Can you answer useful questions?" asked the Red Queen. "How is bread made?"

"I know _that_!" Alice cried eagerly. "You take some flour——"

"Where do you pick the flower?" the White Queen asked. "In a garden, or in the hedges?"

"Well, it isn't _picked_ at all," Alice explained: "it's _ground_ ——"

"How many acres of ground?" said the White Queen. "You mustn't leave out so many things."

"Fan her head!" the Red Queen anxiously interrupted. "She'll be feverish after so much thinking." So they set to work and fanned her with bunches of leaves, till she had to beg them to leave off, it blew her hair about so.

"Do you know Languages?" asked the Red Queen. "What's the French for 'fiddle-de-dee?'"

"Fiddle-de-dee's not English," Alice replied gravely.

"Who ever said it was?" said the Red Queen

Alice thought she saw a way out of the difficulty this time. "If you'll tell me what language 'fiddle-de-dee' is, I'll tell you the French for it!" she exclaimed triumphantly.

But the Red Queen drew herself up rather stiffly, and said "Queens never make bargains."

"I wish Queens never asked questions," Alice thought to herself.

"Don't let us quarrel," the White Queen said in an anxious tone. She gave a deep sigh, and laid her head on Alice's shoulder.

"I _am_ so sleepy," she moaned.

"She's tired, poor thing!" said the Red Queen. "Smooth her hair——lend her your nightcap——and sing her a soothing lullaby."

"I haven't got a nightcap with me," said Alice, as she tried to obey the first direction: "and I don't know any soothing lullabies."

"I must do it myself, then," said the Red Queen, and she began:

"Hush-a-by lady, in Alice's lap!
Till the feast's ready, we've time for a nap:
When the feast's over, we'll go to the ball ——
Red Queen, and White Queen, and Alice, and all!

"And now you know the words," she added, as she put her head down on Alice's other shoulder, "just sing it through to _me_. I'm getting sleepy, too." In another moment both

Queens were fast asleep, and snoring loud.

"What _am_ I to do?" exclaimed Alice, looking about in great perplexity, as first one round head, and then the other, rolled down from her shoulder, and lay like a heavy lump in her lap. "Do wake up, you heavy things!" she went on in an impatient tone; but there was no answer but a gentle snoring.

The snoring got more distinct every minute, and sounded more like a tune: at last she could even make out the words, and she listened so eagerly that, when the two great heads vanished from her lap, she hardly missed them.

She was standing before an arched doorway over which were the words QUEEN ALICE in large letters, and on each side of the arch there was a bell-handle; one was marked 'Visitors' Bell,' and the other 'Servants' Bell.'

"I'll wait till the song's over," thought Alice, "and then I'll ring—the—_which_ bell must I ring?" she went on, very much puzzled. "I'm not a visitor, and I'm not a servant.

There ought to be one marked 'Queen,' you know —"

At this moment the door was flung open, and loud voices were heard singing:

"To the Looking-Glass world it was Alice that said,
'I've a sceptre in hand, I've a crown on my head;
Let the Looking-Glass creatures, whatever they be,
Come dine with the Red Queen, the White Queen, & me.'
Then fill up the glasses as quick as you can,
And sprinkle the table with buttons and bran:
Put cats in the coffee, and mice in the tea —
And welcome Queen Alice with thirty-times-three!
'O Looking-Glass creatures,' quoth Alice, 'draw near!
'Tis an honour to see me, a favour to hear:
'Tis a privilege high to have dinner and tea
Along with the Red Queen, the White Queen, & me!'
Then fill up the glasses with treacle and ink,
Or anything else that is pleasant to drink:
Mix sand with the cider, and wool with the wine —
And welcome Queen Alice with ninety-times-nine!"

"Ninety times nine!" Alice repeated in despair, "Oh, that'll never be done! I'd better go in at once ———" and there was a dead silence the moment she appeared.

Alice glanced nervously along the table, as she walked up the large hall, and noticed that there were about fifty guests, of all kinds: some were animals, some birds, and there were even a few flowers among them. "I'm glad they've come without waiting to be asked," she thought: "I should never have known who were the right people to invite!"

There were three chairs at the head of the table; the Red and White Queens had already taken two of them, but the middle one was empty. Alice sat down in it, rather uncomfortable in the silence, and longing for someone to speak.

At last the Red Queen began. "You've missed the soup and fish," she said. "Put on the joint!" And the waiters set a leg of mutton before Alice, who looked at it rather anxiously, as she had never had to carve a joint before.

"You look a little shy; let me introduce you to that leg of mutton," said the Red Queen. "Alice —— Mutton; Mutton —— Alice." The leg of mutton

got up in the dish and made a little bow to Alice; and Alice returned the bow, not knowing whether to be frightened or amused.

"May I give you a slice?" she said, taking up the knife and fork, and looking from one Queen to the other.

"Certainly not," the Red Queen said, very decidedly: "it isn't etiquette to cut any one you've been introduced to. Remove the joint!" And the waiters carried it off, and brought a large plum-pudding in its place.

"I won't be introduced to the pudding, please," Alice said rather hastily, "or we shall get no dinner at all. May I give you some?"

But the Red Queen looked sulky, and growled "Pudding — Alice; Alice —— Pudding. Remove the pudding!" and the waiters took it away so quickly that Alice couldn't return its bow.

However, she didn't see why the Red Queen should be the only one to give orders, so, as an experiment, she called out "Waiter! Bring back the pudding!" and there it was again in a moment like a conjuring-trick. She cut a slice and handed it to the Red Queen.

"What impertinence!" said the Pudding. "I wonder how you'd like it, if I were to cut a slice out of _you_, you creature!"

It spoke in a thick, suety sort of voice, and Alice hadn't a word to say in reply: she could only sit and look at it and gasp.

"Make a remark," said the Red Queen: "it's ridiculous to leave all the conversation to the pudding! Meanwhile, we'll drink your health——Queen Alice's health!" she screamed at the top of her voice, and all the guests began drinking noisily.

"You ought to return thanks in a neat speech," the Red Queen said, frowning at Alice as she spoke.

"I rise to return thanks ——" Alice began: and she really _did_ rise as she spoke, several inches; but she got hold of the edge of the table, and managed to pull herself down again.

"Take care of yourself!" screamed the White Queen, seizing Alice's hair with both her hands. "Something's going to happen!"

And then all sorts of things happened in a moment. The candles all grew up to the ceiling, looking something like a bed of rushes with fire-works at the top. The bottles each took a pair of plates as wings, and so, with forks for legs, went fluttering about in all directions.

There was not a moment to be lost. Already several of the guests were lying down in the dishes, and the soup-ladle was walking up the table towards Alice's chair, and beckoning to her impatiently to get out of its way.

"I ca'n't stand this any longer!" she cried as she jumped up and seized the table-cloth with both hands: one good pull, and plates, dishes, guests, and candles came crashing down together in a heap on the floor.

"And as for <u>you</u>," she went on, turning fiercely upon the Red Queen, whom she considered as the cause of all the mischief — but the Queen had suddenly dwindled down to the size of a little doll.

"As for <u>you</u>," she repeated, catching hold of the little creature, "I'll shake you into a kitten, that I will!"

# Chapter X
# Waking

Alice shook the Red Queen with all her might. The Queen made no resistance whatever; only her eyes got large and green: and as Alice went on shaking her, she kept on growing shorter — and fatter — and softer — and rounder — until it really <u>was</u> a kitten, after all.

# Chapter XI
# Whose Dream Was It?

"Your Majesty shouldn't purr so loud," Alice said, rubbing her eyes. "You woke me out of oh! such a strange dream!"

Alice hunted among the chessmen on the table till she had found the Red Queen: then she went down on her knees on the hearth-rug, and put the kitten and the Queen to look at each other. "Now, Kitty!" she cried, clapping her hands triumphantly. "Confess that was what you turned into!"

The kitten only purred in reply: so it was impossible to guess what it meant.

"Snowdrop, my pet!" she went on, looking

over her shoulder at the white kitten, which was still patiently undergoing its toilet, "when _will_ Dinah have finished with your White Majesty, I wonder? That must be the reason you were so untidy in my dream —— Dinah! do you know that you're scrubbing the White Queen?

"Now, Kitty, let's consider who it was that dreamt it all. This is a serious question, my dear, and you should _not_ go on licking your paw like that! You see, Kitty, it _must_ have been either me or the Red King. He was part of my dream, of course —— but then I was part of his dream, too! _Was_ it the Red King, Kitty? You were his wife, my dear, so you ought to know —— Oh, Kitty, _do_ help to settle it! I'm sure your paw can wait!" But the provoking kitten only began on the other paw, and pretended it hadn't heard the question.

Which do _you_ think it was?

A boat beneath a sunny sky,
Lingering onward dreamily
In an evening of July —
Children three that nestle near,
Eager eye and willing ear,
Pleased a simple tale to hear —
Long has paled that sunny sky:
Echoes fade and memories die.
Autumn frosts have slain July.
Still she haunts me, phantomwise,
Alice moving under skies
Never seen by waking eyes.
Children yet, the tale to hear,
Eager eye and willing ear,
Lovingly shall nestle near.
In a Wonderland they lie,
Dreaming as the days go by,
Dreaming as the summers die:
Ever drifting down the stream —
Lingering in the golden gleam —
Life, what is it but a dream?

## THE END

Looking
Glass
House

# Behind *Looking-Glass House*

Lewis Carroll wrote out *Through the Looking-Glass* by hand – typewriters were not yet a household item in the late 1860s – as a guide for the printer, but that manuscript did not survive. And it was very unlikely to have included illustrations, so we have no drawings by Carroll to suggest what he thought his *Looking-Glass* characters should look like.

At the Alice150 gathering in New York in 2015, Mark Richards, a former president of the Lewis Carroll Society in England, remarked to me how thrilling it would be if a long-lost manuscript version of *Through the Looking-Glass* were to be discovered in a dusty trunk somewhere. I replied that I'd want a facsimile of such a thing, even if it was a fake. *Even if it was a fake? That's ridiculous!* Of course someone could create a fake, using a "Lewis Carroll font" to make the lettering look authentic and drawing new illustrations in the style of Dodgson's quaint, charmingly crude pictures in *Alice's Adventures under Ground.* But if it were nothing but a fake, why would anyone care?

Maybe it was the wine talking, but I still wanted one, and so did Mark Richards. I couldn't get the idea out my mind. So I decided to assemble a creative team to design and publish an imaginary "rough draft" manuscript, one that Lewis Carroll might have presented to Alice Liddell, had she "left off at seven" instead of rudely growing up. (Alice was nineteen when *Through the Looking-Glass* was published. Her intimate friendship with Carroll had long since dissolved, though he thoughtfully gave her a specially bound and signed copy of the book when it came out in 1871. And he secretly dedicated the book to Alice Pleasance Liddell by encoding her name into an acrostic that's easily visible in the book's final poem.)

Artist Jonathan David Dixon took on the extraordinary task of creating thirty-three new illustrations in the amateurish style of Lewis Carroll. With Mark Burstein acting as editor and advisor and Andrew Ogus as book designer, I took it upon myself to adapt the text. We were lucky to have Matthew Demakos's article "The Authentic Wasp" in the Lewis Carroll Society of North America's terrific journal *Knight Letter* (#72, Winter 2003), which contains many intriguing clues about how *Through the Looking-Glass* evolved, including reproducing an early draft of a table of contents (from Harvard University's Houghton Library archive) with Carroll's ideas about the book's and its chapters' original titles.

We've crafted, we hope, a fit companion to *Alice's Adventures under Ground* of which Lewis Carroll himself might approve – lovingly created in memory of a special friendship that inspired magical stories born of magical summer days.

– Daniel Rover Singer, 2016